Beetle
and the
Big Tree

Beetle and Friends

**Get together with Beetle
and his friends!**

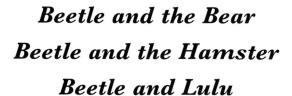

Be sure to read:
Beetle and the Bear
Beetle and the Hamster
Beetle and Lulu
... and lots, lots more!

Beetle
and the
Big Tree

Hilary McKay
illustrated by Lesley Harker

For Kevin with love – H.M. and Jim

This edition produced for the Book People Ltd,
Hall Wood Avenue, Haydock, St Helens WA11 9UL

First published by Scholastic Ltd, 2002

ISBN 0 439 95439 8

Printed and bound by Tien Wah Press Pte. Ltd, Singapore

Beetle and Max lived in a very small house with a long, narrow garden. At the bottom of the garden was a broken down fence. On the other side of the fence was an enormous tree.

The cedar tree
had giant-sized
branches that
filled the sky.
It grew in the
garden of the
Big House,
where no one had
lived for years and
years. Ever since
he could remember
Beetle had wanted
to climb it.

6

"Do you think anyone has ever climbed it before?" he asked his brother Max.

"No," said Max. "It's much too difficult."

"That means we will be the first," said Beetle happily.

The reason the
tree was so hard
to climb was that
the first branch
was so high.

Beetle and Max
had tried to
reach it using
the kitchen steps.

They had fallen
off so many
times they had
worn away the
grass underneath.

Then Beetle had his brilliant idea. It came one day when he was holding the steps while Max balanced on tiptoe at the top.

"The biscuit tin!" he cried, letting go of the steps, so that Max fell off them once again.

"Ouch!" said Max, but Beetle had gone.

"It's just
what we
need!"
he said,
when he came puffing back.

Beetle was right. With the biscuit tin on
top of the steps and someone on top of the
biscuit tin they were high enough to reach
the first branch. Beetle had just got his arms
right round it when their mother called
from the house,
"Bedtime!"

Beetle dropped quickly to the ground, before she saw that they had nearly managed to get into the tree at last.

"I almost did it," he whispered excitedly to Max.

"We will next time," promised Max.

Chapter Two

Then something terrible happened. The
Big House was sold and people moved in.
One day Beetle came home from school to
find a new wooden fence across the end of
the garden. The cedar tree was on the
other side.

"We'll have to climb over the fence," said Max.

"No climbing anywhere in those clothes," said their mother. "Run upstairs and get changed, and I'm sorry boys, you will have to find somewhere different to play."

Beetle and Max went upstairs. From their bedroom window they could look across to the cedar tree.

Beetle stared out of the window for a long time and rubbed his eyes and sniffed. Then he saw someone crossing the Big House garden.

It was the new boy who had been at school that day. His name was Oswald but everyone called him the Rich Kid.

The Rich Kid was wheeling a shiny red bike. Beetle and Max watched him prop it carefully against the trunk of the cedar tree and climb up until he was standing on the saddle.

"I'm going
to stop him!"
exclaimed
Beetle.

He ran out of the bedroom, down the
stairs, into the garden and yelled,
"Hey! What do you think you're
doing? That's our tree!"

"It's not," said the Rich
Kid calmly. "It's
ours. I'm going
to climb it."

"Max and me have been going to climb that tree for years and years and years!" said Beetle, furiously.

"Why didn't you then?" asked the Rich Kid.

Chapter Three

From that day on Beetle and Max and the
Rich Kid were enemies. Beetle and Max
had never had an enemy before. It made
them feel awful. They hated it.

Every day the Rich Kid would come home from school and try and climb the cedar tree.

Over and over again he crashed to the ground with his bike on top of him.

Beetle and Max hung over the new fence and watched.

Sometimes they spoke to him.

"Where's your mum and dad?"

"Work."

"Who's in the house then?"

"Mrs Silver. She comes in to clean and do stuff."

"What's she doing now?"

"I expect she's cooking my tea."

"You'll ruin that bike."

"I've got other bikes."

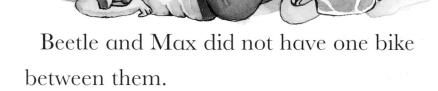

Beetle and Max did not have one bike between them.

"Why don't you go to a Rich Kids' school?" asked Beetle rudely.

"Why don't you," said the Rich Kid slowly, "go to a Nosy Neighbour Big Wet Baby Rotten Horrible Jealous Kids' School?"

He looked the way he did at school when they were picking teams for football and he knew he would be left out.

Suddenly Max felt a little sorry for him, and when Beetle opened his mouth to be even ruder, he said, "Shut up, Beetle!"

The Rich Kid
pretended to ignore
them both. He climbed
on to his bike again,
reached up, gripped the
branch, and kicked
off harder than he
ever had before.

Crash! went the bike as the Rich Kid's
legs swung high into the air. His feet
grabbed the first branch of the cedar tree
and he hung upside down.

A moment later he got a knee on to the branch. Then he was sitting with a leg each side of it, laughing with triumph.

"I did it!" he called.

Beetle found he had been holding his breath. He let it out with a whoosh. If they had not been enemies he would have cheered. He would have shouted, "Brilliant, Os!"

But he did not say anything, and neither did Max.

The Rich Kid stopped laughing. He looked down at Beetle and Max, who had not managed one friendly word, and he said, "You'd never have made it in a thousand years!"

Beetle and Max turned away and went into the house.

Chapter Four

The next day the Rich Kid got into the
cedar tree again. And the next day, and the
next. Every day he got a little higher than
the day before. One day, when he saw
Beetle looking at him, he called, "Want to
watch me climb my tree? You'd never have
made it in a million years!"

Beetle stamped off to find Max, who was doing his homework.

"That Rich Kid is halfway up our cedar tree now," he told him.

"Are you sure?" asked Max.

"I saw him," said Beetle. "It's not fair. We were going to climb it first. He said we'd never have made it in a million years! Well, we'll show him!"

"How?"

"We'll climb it
ourselves!" said
Beetle. "We'll do
it really early,
while everyone
is still asleep. We'll
get to the top
before he does!"

Beetle began to bounce up and down
with excitement.

"We'll stick a message on the highest
branch! Like a flag!"

Max began to laugh.

"We can set the alarm on your watch to wake us!" said Beetle. "Tomorrow, before anyone else is up!"

"All right," said Max.

Chapter Five

The next morning Beetle and Max were
awake at dawn. Beetle collected the
flag he had made with
a pillowcase and
felt pen writing.

BEETLE
WAS
HERE!

Quietly they crept downstairs and
gathered up the steps and the biscuit tin
from the kitchen.

Then they unlocked the back door,
sneaked down the garden, and climbed over
the fence.

Beetle laid his cheek against the trunk of the tree and whispered, "We've come back."

Then they began to climb. Max went first, launching himself from the biscuit tin on to the first branch.

Then, with Max helping from above, Beetle heaved himself up as well.

"At last! At last!"
said Beetle.

They set off
further into the
tree. It was not so
hard for them as it
had been for the Rich

Kid because he had been climbing alone.
Two people together could help each other.

As they went higher
the branches grew
closer together,
and it became
almost easy.

They felt as if they could carry on for ever.

After a while Beetle stopped to admire the view.

"There's our cat," he said.

The cat was on their bedroom window sill. She was looking up at them. She looked very small.

"This tree is higher than our house," said Max.

"Yes," said Beetle, and he glanced up. They were very near the top. A little breeze had begun to blow.

Beetle noticed then that the tree was moving. It gave him a tingly, cold feeling, all down his spine.

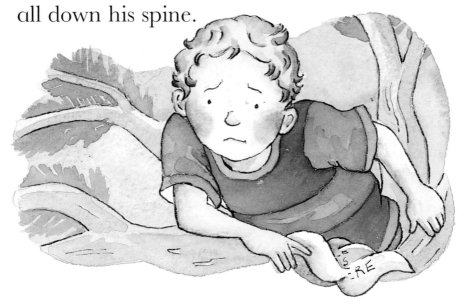

"Only a little way more," he said to Max, but he did not move. Instead he clung on tightly with his hands and knees and tried to concentrate on the cat.

"I don't know how she can bear to sit there," he said shakily.

Just as if she had heard him, the cat stood up, stretched lazily along the narrow sill, and jumped.

That made Beetle and Max look down, and they saw just how far away the ground was. It was like looking through the wrong end of a telescope. It made their knees shake, and their stomachs turn, and their heads feel light and swimmy.

"I'm going to fall!"
wailed Beetle.
"Max, Max!
I'm going
to fall!"

Max said,
"You're not
going to fall,"
but his voice
was strange
and high.

39

Then Beetle accidentally let go of his pillowcase flag and it floated like a feather, all the way to the ground.

"Max! Max!" cried Beetle.

Chapter Six

In his sleep Oswald heard Beetle's cry. He rolled out of bed and went to the window and looked out. First he saw the kitchen steps and the biscuit tin and the fallen flag. Then he saw Beetle and Max high in the tree, hanging on for their lives.

Oswald forgot
that Max and
Beetle were
his enemies.
He flew
down the
stairs, out
of the house
and straight up

on to the first branch of the cedar tree.

"Hold on! Hold on!" he cried, as he

swung himself up through the branches,

faster than he
had ever
climbed
before.

Looking at Oswald instead of looking at
the ground made Beetle and Max begin to
feel better. Their dizzy feelings faded away.

"Hold on!" called Oswald. "I'm coming!"

Just as he said that they saw him slip. He
lost his grip and began to fall.

Oswald slid tumbling and grabbing from branch to branch, faster and faster.

The branches shook as he hit them. Beetle shut his eyes because he could not bear to look.

There was a sound like a horrible crunch. Beetle opened his eyes and there was Oswald, spread out like a starfish on the grass below.

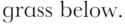

Beetle plunged
down the cedar
tree almost as fast as
Oswald had fallen,
reaching and
swinging, calling,
"Os! Os!"

He came to the last branch, let go, and
landed.

Oswald's eyes were shut.

Max dropped down beside Beetle.

"Os!" whispered Beetle, and he mopped Oswald's head with the pillowcase flag.

Oswald opened his eyes.

"Don't try to move!" ordered Max.

"Os," said Beetle. "That awful crunch. Have you... Did you... What was it, Os?"

Oswald sat up and moved backwards. He pulled something out from underneath him. It was the biscuit tin, squashed flat.

Then he lay down again and began to shake with laughter.

Beetle and Max began to laugh too. They laughed until they were weak. They laughed until it hurt. It was so good to not be enemies at last.

"What was it like at the top?" asked Oswald.

"Awful," said Beetle, and they began to laugh again.

They ate up all the biscuits, even the ones squashed almost to crumbs.

"Os," said Beetle. "Have you really got more than one bike?"

"I've got three," said Os, but he did not say it like a Rich Kid. He just said it like a boy with a lot of bikes.

"We can ride one each," said Os.